Graphic Organizers in Science™

Learning About Force and Motion with Graphic Organizers

Julie Fiedler

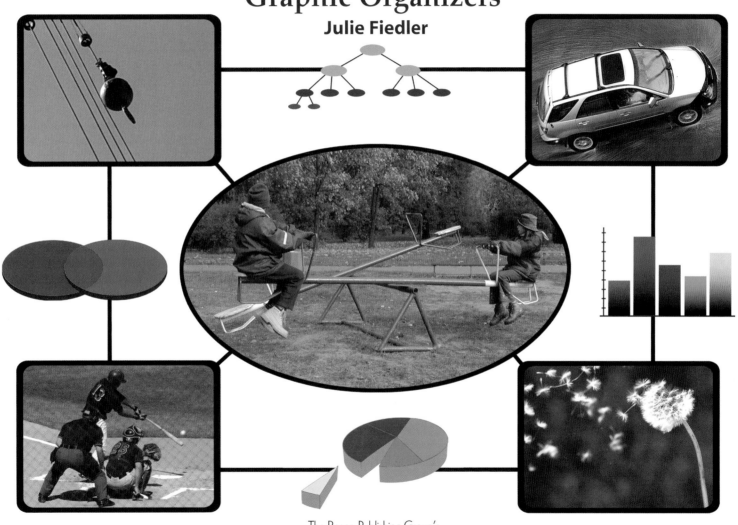

The Rosen Publishing Group's
PowerKids Press™
New York

For my teachers, with gratitude

Published in 2007 by The Rosen Publishing Group, Inc.
29 East 21st Street, New York, NY 10010

First Edition

Editor: Jennifer Way
Layout Design: Julio A. Gil

Photo Credits: Cover & title page (center), p. 4 (bottom left) © www.istockphoto.com/Andrzej Tokarski; cover & title page (top left), p. 4 (top left) ©www.istockphoto.com/Frances Twitty; cover & title page (top right), p. 4 (top right) © www.istockphoto.com/Michael Gomez; cover & title page (bottom left), p. 4 (bottom center) © www.istockphoto.com/Michael Blanc; cover & title page (bottom right), p. 4 (top center) © www.istockphoto.com/Joshua Sowin; p. 4 (bottom right) © www.istockphoto.com/Bill Grove; p. 7 © Corbis; p. 8 (Aristotle, Copernicus, Newton) Images copyright History of Science Collections, University of Oklahoma Libraries; p. 8 (Ptolemy, Galileo) Library of Congress Prints and Photographs Division; pp. 12, 20 © PhotoDisc; p. 20 (top right) © Royalty Free/Corbis.

Library of Congress Cataloging-in-Publication Data

Fiedler, Julie.
  Learning about force and motion with graphic organizers / Julie Fiedler.— 1st ed.
      p. cm. — (Graphic organizers in science)
  Includes index.
  ISBN 1-4042-3410-1 (library binding)
  1. Force and energy—Study and teaching (Elementary)—Graphic methods—Juvenile literature. 2. Motion—Study and teaching (Elementary)—Graphic methods—Juvenile literature. I. Title. II. Series.
  QC73.4.F54 2007
  372.35—dc22

                              2005028985

Manufactured in the United States of America

Contents

Concept Web: Forces That Cause Motion

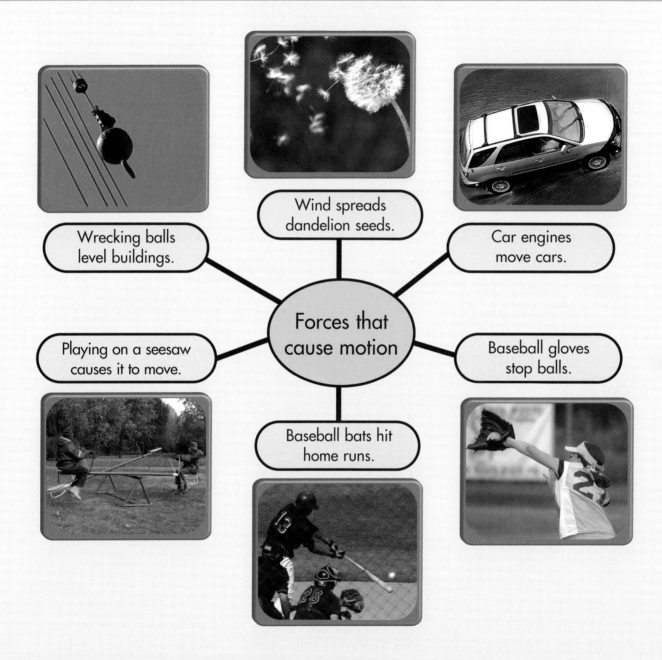

Wrecking balls level buildings.

Wind spreads dandelion seeds.

Car engines move cars.

Forces that cause motion

Playing on a seesaw causes it to move.

Baseball gloves stop balls.

Baseball bats hit home runs.

Force and Motion

Force is a push or a pull that has a direction, such as a push away or a pull toward something. Force acts on an object at rest and makes it move. Motion is movement, or the change in an object's position over time.

A person can push very hard on a heavy object and not move it. A person can create a force, but if the object has a stronger force, the object will not move. Once an object starts to move, it will continue moving until another force acts on it to stop it. Its continuing motion is called **momentum**.

One example of force is the game tug-of-war. Two teams hold opposite ends of a rope and pull as hard as they can in opposite directions. The team with greater force will cause the rope to move toward that side and win the game.

A concept web is a graphic organizer with a main subject in the middle. Facts and examples are added around the subject. You can add more facts as you learn about the subject. This concept web shows different examples of forces that cause motion.

Measuring Motion

There are several different ways to measure motion. Distance tells you how far something moves. To measure distance you mark the point where the object started moving and the point where the object stopped moving. A ruler can show you that a snail moved 3 inches (8 cm). An **odometer** in a car measures larger distances, such as miles (km). Because motion is a change in position over time, you can also measure speed. The distance traveled and the amount of time it takes together give you the speed. A car's speed is measured in miles per hour (km/h).

Another motion measurement is called **acceleration**. Acceleration measures the rate of speed. If it takes a car 1 minute to go from rest to traveling 60 miles per hour (97 km/h), then the car's acceleration is 60 miles per hour (97 km/h) per minute.

This graphic organizer is called a flow chart. On this flow chart, you can see how different amounts of force act on an object.

Flow Chart: Force

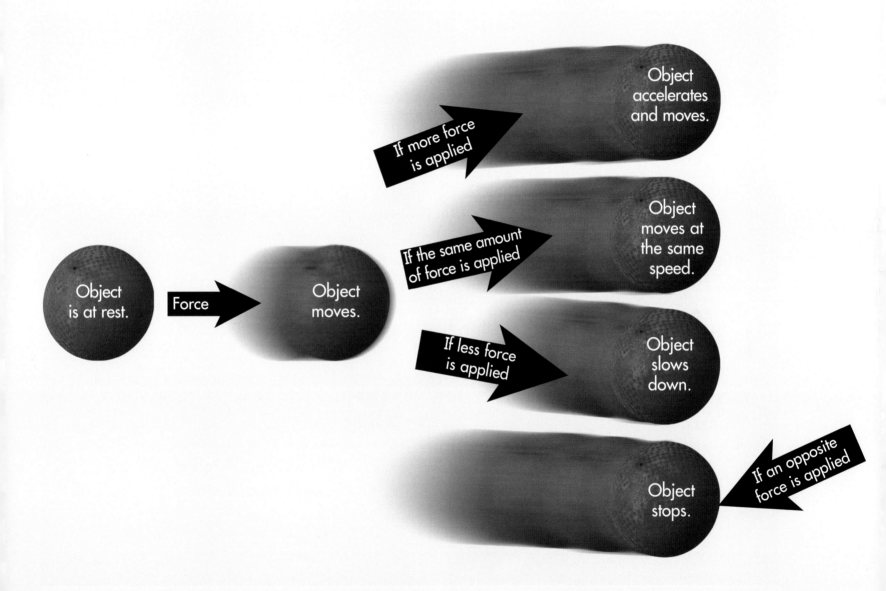

Object is at rest.

Force →

Object moves.

If more force is applied → Object accelerates and moves.

If the same amount of force is applied → Object moves at the same speed.

If less force is applied → Object slows down.

If an opposite force is applied → Object stops.

Timeline: Scientific Theories About Force and Motion

Aristotle: Earth does not move. Incorrect.

Objects naturally slow down without a force acting on them. Incorrect.

A.D. 150s

Ptolemy: Earth is at the center of the universe. Incorrect.

1500s

Copernicus: The Sun is at the center of the universe, or all of space. Incorrect.

1630s

Galileo Galilei: More than one force can act on an object at once. Correct.

Objects move forever unless another force acts on them. Correct.

1680s

Isaac Newton: Laws of gravity. Correct.

Objects close to Earth fall at the same speed. Correct.

Laws of motion. Correct.

Earth moves around the Sun. Correct.

Measuring Force

Scientists use **newtons** to measure force. One newton will move an object that weighs 2.2 pounds (1 kg) a distance of 3.3 feet (1 m) per second each second. The newton combines the measurements of weight of an object and its acceleration.

Scientists measure force using a spring balance. This tool has a spring inside and numbered markings on the outside. The spring **stretches,** or contracts, based on the force. As the spring stretches or contracts, a pointer moves along the numbered markings. When the pointer is at marker 3, the force is 3 newtons. You can see the strength of different forces using rubber bands, which stretch and contract like springs. More force is needed to stretch a rubber band 6 inches (15 cm) than is needed to stretch it 3 inches (8 cm).

This graphic organizer is a timeline. Timelines show the order in which events happened. This timeline shows the theories, or ideas, of scientists who studied force. We know today that some of these theories were incorrect. The incorrect theories are labeled on the timeline.

Friction

Pushing and pulling are the two main forces. Another common force is called **friction**. Friction is a force that occurs between the surfaces of two or more objects. A smooth surface creates little friction and does not slow an object down much. An uneven surface creates more friction and slows objects down more.

To see friction in action, roll a ball across a wooden floor. Then roll the same ball using the same force across a rug. The ball will roll farther and faster across the wooden floor. That is because there is less friction on the floor to slow it down. Roll a heavier ball using the same force across the same surfaces. You will see that the heavier ball does not roll as far as the lighter ball. The weight of the heavier ball pushes down. This makes the surfaces stick together more and causes more friction.

A bar graph shows values of different things so you can compare and contrast. This bar graph shows different levels of friction between everyday objects. The numbers on the left show the amount of friction when the objects are rubbed together. The higher the number, the more friction is created.

Bar Graph: Friction in Everyday Objects

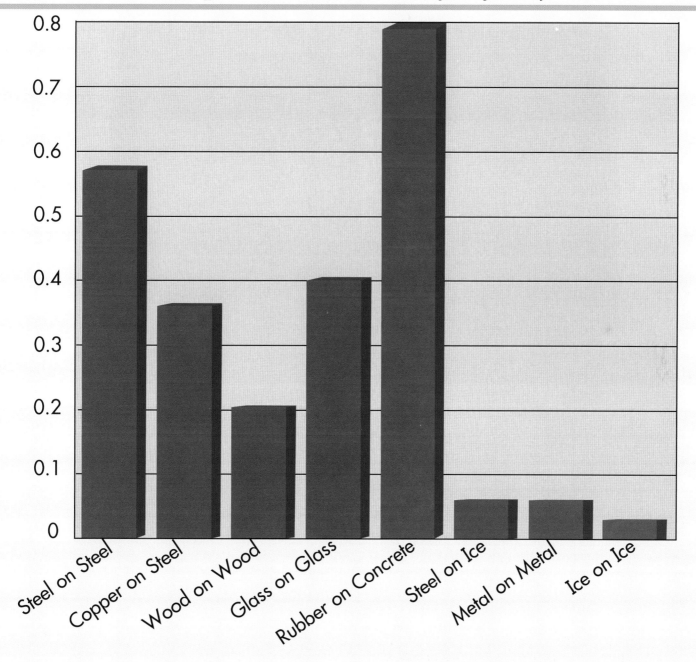

11

Compare/Contrast: Weight and Gravity

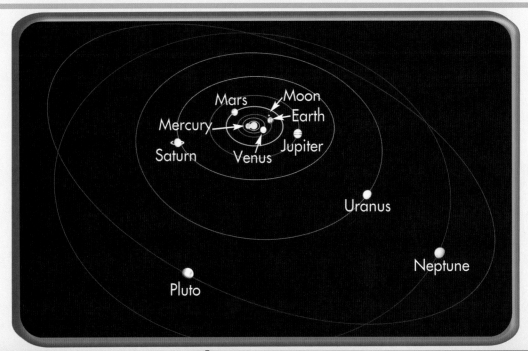

Location	Mass	Gravity	Weight (lbs)	Weight (kgs)
Mercury	95	0.4	36.1	16.3
Venus	95	0.9	85.5	38.5
Earth	95	1	95	42.8
The Moon	95	0.2	16.2	7.3
Mars	95	0.4	36.1	16.3
Jupiter	95	2.4	224.2	100.9
Saturn	95	0.92	87.4	39.3
Uranus	95	0.89	84.6	38.1
Neptune	95	1.1	107.4	48.3
Pluto	95	0.07	6.7	3.0
Outer Space	95	0	0	0.00

Gravity

If you hold an object in your hand and let it go, the object will drop toward the earth. This is because of **gravity**. The gravity of Earth is a pull that draws everything toward the ground. Gravity is what gives objects weight. Even though objects have different weights, gravity pulls them down at the same rate of acceleration.

When people went to the Moon, they tested its gravity by dropping a feather and a hammer at the same time. The feather and the hammer hit the surface of the Moon at the same time. This is because the Moon has no air, so there is no air **resistance**. Air resistance is another type of force that slows objects down. The feather and the hammer also took longer to drop on the Moon than on Earth. This is because the force of the Moon's gravity is less than the force of gravity on Earth.

Compare/contrast charts show what is the same and what is different among two or more subjects. This chart shows the differences between the gravity and the weight of a 95-pound (42.8 kg) person on different planets. To figure out your weight on different planets, multiply your weight, which is the same as mass, and the gravity of the different planets.

Laws of Motion

Isaac Newton wrote the three laws of motion that explained why objects move the way they do. Newton's first law of motion states that an object will not start or stop moving without a force acting on it. This law is called the law of **inertia**.

Newton's second law of motion states that the acceleration of an object is based on its mass and the force applied to it. This means that if a large force is applied to a small object, the object will accelerate quickly.

Newton's third law is often stated as, "For every force there is an equal and opposite force." For example, if you stand still on a skateboard and throw a ball forward, the force you used to throw the ball will also push you backward on the skateboard.

A tree chart shows the subject of the graphic organizer in the trunk. Elements of the subject are added as branches. This chart shows Newton's laws of motion.

Tree Chart: Newton's Laws of Motion

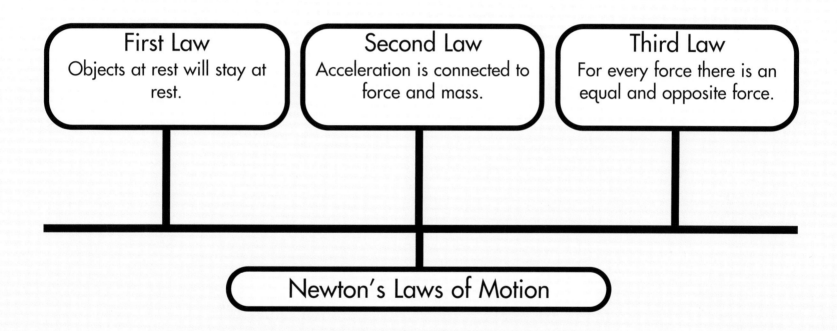

First Law
Objects at rest will stay at rest.

Second Law
Acceleration is connected to force and mass.

Third Law
For every force there is an equal and opposite force.

Newton's Laws of Motion

Line Graph: Combined Forces

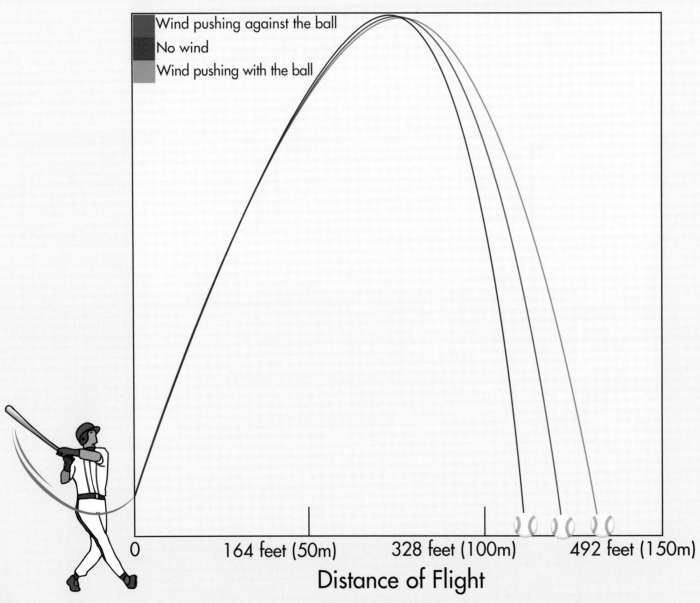

Wind pushing against the ball
No wind
Wind pushing with the ball

0   164 feet (50m)   328 feet (100m)   492 feet (150m)

Distance of Flight

Combined Forces

More than one force is usually acting on an object. This creates what is called a combined force, or a **resultant force**. For example, when you throw a ball, the forward force of your throw and the downward force of gravity both act on the ball. This combined force makes the ball move in a curve.

Sometimes combined forces move in the same direction, which makes the resultant force bigger. Let's say two people push a box in the same direction with the same force. The resultant force is the sum of their two forces acting together.

Another combination of forces occurs when there is a **collision**. When playing the game of pool you hit the white ball toward the colored balls. The force of the moving white ball collides with the resting colored balls. They then break apart.

This is a line graph. It shows how the combined forces of a throw, gravity, and the wind have an effect on how far a baseball travels.

Circular and Spiral Motion

When an object moves along a path shaped like a circle, it has **circular** motion. An object moving inward along a **spiral** path has spiral motion. An example of circular motion can be seen when you have an object connected to a string and you spin the string in circles. If you spin it fast enough, the object moves in a circle. The force of the string draws the object into the center. If you let go of the string, the object will fly outward. This is because **centripetal force** kept the object on the circular path.

If the force moving an object in a spiral is stopped, it will not fly off in a straight line. It will continue spiraling in. The centripetal force continues to pull it inward. The force gets stronger toward the center.

This graphic organizer is a Venn diagram. It organizes facts to show you what things have in common and what their differences are.

Venn Diagram: Circular Motion and Spiral Motion

Circular Motion

Spiral Motion

- The object moves away from the center.

- Momentum causes the object to move in a straight line if the force stops.

- Round motion.

- Momentum does not change unless force acts on it.

- Centripetal force draws the object in.

- Force increases toward the center.

- Speed increases toward the center.

- The object moves toward the center.

- Momentum causes the object to continue moving in a spiral if the force stops.

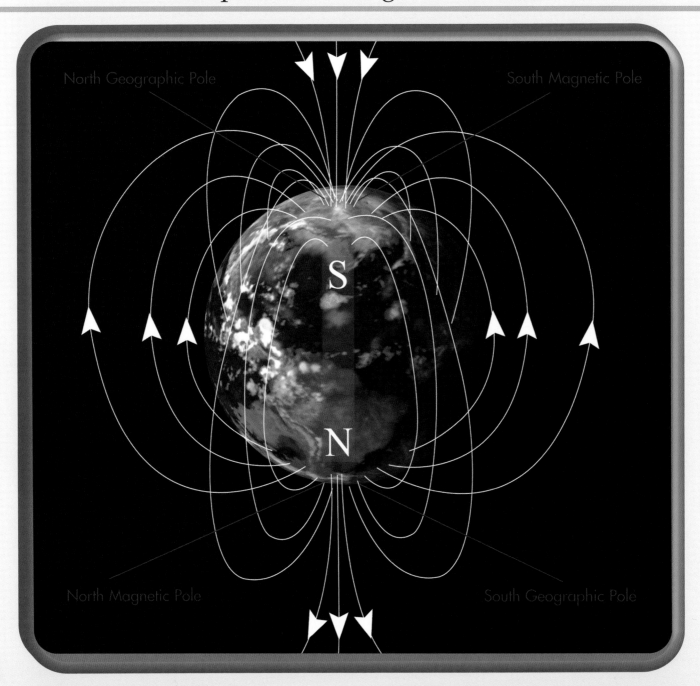

North Geographic Pole

South Magnetic Pole

S

N

North Magnetic Pole

South Geographic Pole

Electric and Magnetic Forces

Electric and magnetic forces are two connected forces. Magnets have two poles, called the north pole and the south pole. These are the parts of the magnet with the strongest force. Put two north poles together or two south poles together. The magnetic force will push the poles apart from each other. Put a north pole and a south pole together. The force will pull them together. Magnets are used in **compasses**.

Electric forces are very much like magnetic forces. They are produced when positively and **negatively** charged **particles** interact. Put two positively or negatively charged particles together. They will push apart from each other just as magnets do. If you put a positively and a negatively charged particle together, they will pull toward each other.

This image is a map of Earth's magnetic fields. Like a magnet, Earth has a north pole and a south pole. Notice that the magnetic poles are at opposite ends from Earth's poles. When you use a compass, the north end of the magnet inside the compass is drawn to the south magnetic pole in Earth. This shows you which direction is north on a map.

Force and Motion in Everyday Life

Can you think of ways in which you see the laws of force and motion at work every day? When you feel how heavy an object is, you know that that is the force of gravity at work. You can also see the effect of force if you think about balance. Balance happens when two forces are the same. For example, on a seesaw one person sits at either end. If they weigh the same and do not move, the seesaw will balance in a straight line. If they apply force, the seesaw will tip back and forth.

Think about how different objects require more force to move them. You can begin to understand how tools, such as levers and pulleys, help people move heavy objects. These tools make the force a person applies greater than the force of heavy objects. Now that you know more about force and motion, you can see them at work all around you.

Glossary

acceleration (ek-seh-luh-RAY-shun) An increase in speed.

centripetal force (sen-TRIH-peh-tul FORS) A force that pushes objects moving in a circular path toward the center.

circular (SER-kyuh-ler) Having the form of a circle.

collision (kuh-LIH-zhun) Two or more things hitting each other.

compasses (KUM-pus-ez) Tools made up of freely turning magnetic needles that tell which direction is north.

friction (FRIK-shin) The rubbing of one thing against another.

gravity (GRA-vih-tee) The natural force that causes objects to move toward the center of Earth.

inertia (ih-NER-shuh) The law that says that matter will stay at rest unless a force acts upon it and that matter will stay in motion unless a force acts upon it.

momentum (moh-MEN-tum) Continuing motion.

negatively (NEH-guh-tiv-lee) The opposite of positively.

newtons (NOO-tunz) The scientific measure of force.

odometer (oh-DAH-muh-tur) A tool for measuring distance traveled.

particles (PAR-tih-kulz) Small pieces of things.

resistance (rih-ZIS-tens) A force that works against another force.

resultant force (rih-ZUL-tunt FORS) The product of two forces acting on the same object.

spiral (SPY-rul) Curved.

stretches (STREH-chez) Pulls two things away from each other.

Index

A
acceleration, 6, 9, 13–14

C
centripetal force, 18
circular motion, 18
collision, 17

E
electric forces, 21

G
gravity, 13, 17, 22

I
inertia, 14

L
laws of motion, 14, 22

M
magnetic forces, 21
momentum, 5

N
Newton, Isaac, 14
newtons, 9

O
odometer, 6

R
resistance, 13
resultant force, 17

S
spiral motion, 18
spring balance, 9

Web Sites

Due to the changing nature of Internet links, PowerKids Press has developed an online list of Web sites related to the subject of this book. This site is updated regularly. Please use this link to access the list: www.powerkidslinks.com/gosci/force/